SIKH GURUS

The Lives and Times of the Ten Sikh Gurus

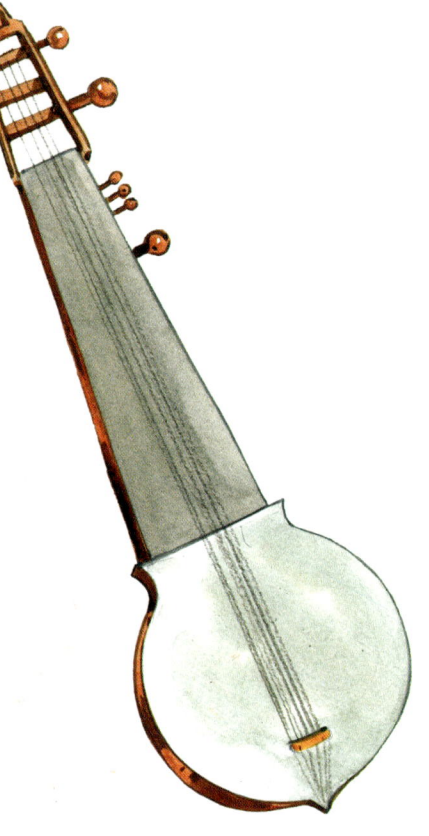

Reprinted in 2016 by

An imprint of Om Books International

Corporate & Editorial Office
A 12, Sector 64, Noida 201 301
Uttar Pradesh, India
Phone: +91 120 477 4100
Email: editorial@ombooks.com
Website: www.ombooksinternational.com

Sales Office
107, Ansari Road, Darya Ganj
New Delhi 110 002, India
Phone: +91 11 4000 9000
Fax: +91 11 2327 8091
Email: sales@ombooks.com
Website: www.ombooks.com

Copyright © Om Books International 2013

Research & Content: Subhojit Sanyal
Illustrations: Manoj Kumar Prasad, Dipankar Mukherjee, Salil Anand

ALL RIGHTS RESERVED. No part of this book may be reproduced or transmitted in any form by any means, electronic or mechanical, including photocopying and recording, or by any information storage and retrieval system, except as may be expressly permitted in writing by the publisher.

ISBN: 978-93-81607-43-5

Printed in India

10 9 8 7 6 5 4 3 2

SIKH GURUS

The Lives and Times of the Ten Sikh Gurus

An imprint of Om Books International

CONTENTS

Guru Nanak　　　　　　　　7

Guru Angad　　　　　　　35

Guru Amar Das　　　　　49

Guru Ram Das　　　　　 57

Guru Arjan Dev　　　　　69

Guru Hargobind   79

Guru Har Rai   86

Guru Har Krishan   94

Guru Teg Bahadur   101

Guru Gobind Singh   110

GURU NANAK

The number of followers of the Sikh faith have grown manifold over time. It is today the fifth-largest organised religion followed around the whole world, with a growing number of people finding inner peace in the teachings of the religion.

According to their religious beliefs, the followers of Sikhism, known as Sikhs, place their complete trust and belief in the Waheguru, or the one God, represented by the phrase "Ik Onkar", whereby they move towards the salvation of the mind, body and soul through disciplined meditation on the name and message of God.

The message of the Sikh faith was first propounded by the founder of the religion, Guru Nanak, way back in the late 15th century and since then, the basic tenets of the religion have been expanded and propounded by the Ten Gurus of Sikhism. The believers in the Sikh faith are all ordained to follow the teachings of these ten gurus — Guru Nanak Dev, Guru Angad Dev, Guru Amar Das, Guru Ram Das, Guru Arjan Dev, Guru Hargobind, Guru Har Rai, Guru Har Krishan, Guru Teg Bahadur and Guru Gobind Singh.

Since the last Guru, Guru Gobind Singh, the holy scripture of the Sikhs, the Guru Granth Sahib has been bestowed the position of the **perpetual Guru** of the Sikhs.

The first Sikh Guru, Guru Nanak Dev is considered to have been born on the 15th of April, 1469, in the village of Rai Bhoi di Talwandi (today known as Nankana Sahib, after Guru Nanak) near modern-day Lahore, in Pakistan. The basis of the date of his birth is on the position of the moon that particular year and therefore, it changes every year.

Guru Nanak was born into the pious Hindu family of Mehta Kalyan Das Bedi, who was commonly known by his friends and family as Kalu Mehta. Nanak's mother was Tripta Devi. He had an elder sister called Bebe Nanaki, who Guru Nanak was extremely close to. His father, Kalu Mehta was the accountant of the income made from agriculture in the village of Talwandi, working for Rai Bullar Bhatti, a Muslim landlord of the area.

Unlike every other child, Guru Nanak came into the world with a smile on his lips. This miracle in itself, proved he was an extraordinary child. As he grew up, Guru Nanak displayed many signs of greatness. For instance, at a very early age, he explained to his teacher how the first alphabet of the Persian language, which resembled the numerical one, actually symbolized the oneness of God.

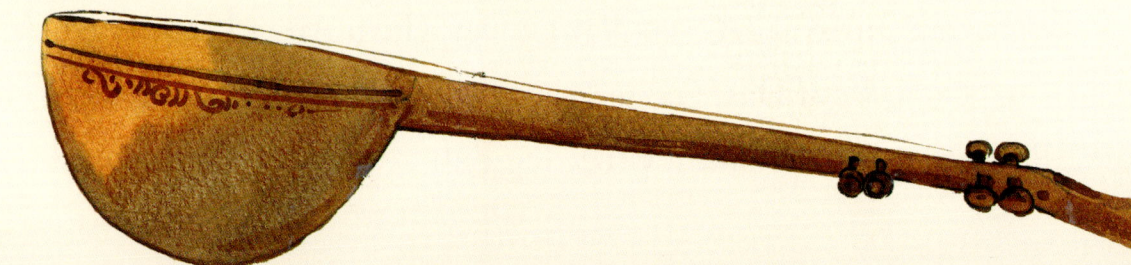

When Nanak was a young boy, his father gave him the job of watching the family's cattle while grazing. As a shepherd, Nanak would sink into deep meditative trances because of which, many times, the cattle would stray into the neighbour's fields, causing damage to their crops. This used to upset his father, though with the passage of time, the villagers started noticing how peaceful Guru Nanak would look when he slipped into these meditative trances and they were slowly convinced that he would go on to be a great saint!

There was also a time when Guru Nanak's father gave him a very small sum of money and asked him to buy some items, which could later be sold for a reasonable profit and be a good bargain (Sacha Sauda). Guru Nanak left for the neighbouring village to carry out his father's instructions. But on the way, he had to cut through a forest, where he saw several ascetics resting in the shade of the forest canopy. Guru Nanak went over and started talking to them, asking them why

they looked so frail. It turned out that the ascetics ate food that was given to them as alms, and had not eaten anything for the past few days. Guru Nanak was greatly saddened on hearing that. He gave the money his father had given him to the ascetics, so that the hungry men could feed themselves. When he returned home, his father was furious with him, but Guru Nanak maintained that he had done what his father had asked him to do — get him a good bargain. Today, the Gurudwara Sacha Sauda stands at the spot where Guru Nanak had conducted this noble "business".

One of the greatest moments in Guru Nanak's life came when his sister, Bebe Nanaki was married to Jai Ram, a steward to Daulat Khan Lodi of Sultanpur, who eventually went on to become the Governor of Lahore. When his sister left for her husband's house in Sultanpur, Guru Nanak, in the traditional Indian practice, accompanied her. On his brother-in-law's advice, Guru Nanak also took up the post of official in charge of the stores of Daulat Khan Lodi. It was there that he first came in contact with Bhai Mardana, a Muslim minstrel, who was much older than Guru Nanak. However, it was Bhai Mardana who could understand the inner doubts and conflicts that Guru Nanak had about religion and beliefs. Together they would discuss these matters and try to find the answers to their questions.

By 1487, Guru Nanak was married to Mata Sulakhni, and soon they were the proud parents of two children — Sri Chand and Lakhmi Chand. Guru Nanak meticulously carried forth his new duties as a husband and a father, but his mind was still in turmoil about the various religions in the world and how they affected people. It was in the year 1499, when Guru Nanak finally saw the light at the end of the tunnel.

One morning, Guru Nanak went to meditate and bathe on the banks of river Kali Bein that flowed through Sultanpur. He never returned home that evening. Anxious friends and family at once started looking for him, but they could find no trace of him. Suddenly, they found his clothes at a spot on the river bank. They

presumed that Guru Nanak had drowned in the river. Daulat Khan Lodi spared no expense in searching along the whole river, but Nanak was nowhere to be found, nor was his body discovered. There was nothing more to be done. So the villagers gave up their search for him.

It was three days later, when everyone was trying to return to their normal lives that Guru Nanak suddenly came back home — as mysteriously as he had disappeared. But Guru Nanak would not speak to anyone, he wouldn't answer anyone's questions about what had happened and where he had gone. It was the next day that he spoke.

"There is neither Hindu or Mussalman (Muslim), but only man. So whose path shall I follow? I shall follow God's path. God is neither a Hindu nor a Mussalman and the path which I follow, is God's."

Guru Nanak declared that four days back, when he was on the bank of the river, he was taken to God's court. There he was offered amrit (nectar) and God said to him, "This is the cup of adoration of

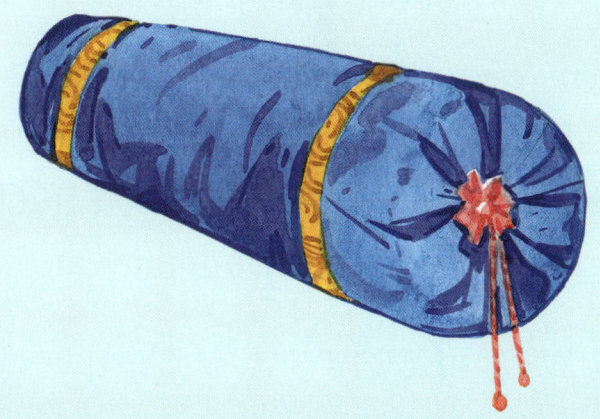

God's name. Drink it, I am with you. I bless you and raise you up. Whoever remembers you will enjoy my favour. Go, rejoice in my name and teach others to do so. I have bestowed the gift of my name upon you. Let this be your calling."

From this point onwards, Nanak was known as Guru Nanak and this was the birth of Sikhism.

Thus enlightened, Guru Nanak gave away all his belongings to the poor, left his family and all worldly pleasures, and along with his spiritual companion, Bhai Mardana, wandered from place to place preaching and teaching that there is but only one God. He went right up to Assam and Bengal in the east, Tamil Nadu in the south, Ladakh, Kashmir and Tibet in the north and to the Arabian Peninsula — Baghdad, Mecca and Medina in the west. He visited all the religious places he could get to and spread the message of God.

It is believed that when Guru Nanak reached Mecca, he decided to rest at the Kaaba mosque. As he slept, his feet were pointing towards the mosque itself. This enraged the chief Muslim cleric, Kaazi Rukan-ud-din, who asked Guru Nanak to turn his feet away and apologise for committing a sin by pointing his feet towards God's abode. Guru Nanak very calmly apologised to the Kaazi first, but then declared that it would be a sin to point his feet in any direction, since every place in this world belonged to God and that He was everywhere. Kaazi Rukan-ud-din was humbled at Guru Nanak's truthful words.

A similar incident happened in Haridwar. Guru Nanak and Bhai Mardana reached Haridwar, one of the holy places on earth for Hindus and saw people dipping their hands in the Ganges and throwing water towards the East, at the rising sun. Guru Nanak could not understand what the people were trying to do, so he asked some of them. He was told that Hindus believed that if they threw the water of the Ganga towards the sun, then the thirst of their deceased ancestors would be quenched in heaven. Without wasting another moment, Guru Nanak too strode into the river, but started throwing water towards the west. Naturally, the shocked people asked him why he was throwing water in the opposite direction. Guru Nanak promptly replied, "If your ancestors can get this water in heaven, I think I can get this water to my home in Punjab. After all, it is a much shorter distance!"

Guru Nanak did not believe in the necessity of creating miracles for people to believe in his words. But according to the legend of Gurudwara Panja Sahib, there was this time in one of his travels that Guru

Nanak did indeed do something miraculous, with the help of divine intervention, to make his followers believe in the word of God.

During his travels westwards in 1521, Guru Nanak reached a place called Hasan Abdal, located around fifty kilometers from Rawalpindi in Pakistan, along with his faithful companion, Bhai Mardana. It being a hot summer day, the two of them took refuge under the shade of a tree, at the foothills of Hasan Abdal. When Guru Nanak and Bhai Mardana started reciting kirtans or holy songs, many people started gathering around them and in no time there was a huge crowd to listen to Guru Nanak who spoke and sang in praise of God and his creation.

An arrogant Muslim priest, by the name of Bawa Wali Qandhari, lived on the top of the hill, near a spring of fresh water. The spring was the only source of water for the town and the people relied on the spring to cater to their needs. The priest was enraged to see the people of the town and from the surrounding villages gather around Guru Nanak

— his heart filled with jealousy to see his followers ignoring him.

In order to teach them all a lesson, he stopped the spring water from flowing down the hill. Left with no water for themselves and their cattle, a group of frustrated men from the town approached Bawa Wali Qandhari and begged him to let the water flow down as before. The furious priest screamed and told them, "Go to your Guru, the one you visit everyday, and ask him for water!" When the people went to Guru Nanak and told him what Qandhari had said, Nanak, in a very calm voice told them to have faith in God. He told them, "Do not be sad. God will not let you die of thirst." Guru Nanak then asked Bhai Mardana to go and request Bawa Wali Qandhari to let the water flow down to the town. However, when Bhai Mardana went to the top of the hill, Bawa Wali Qandhari once again shouted angrily, "Go back to your Guru and ask him to give water to the people!"

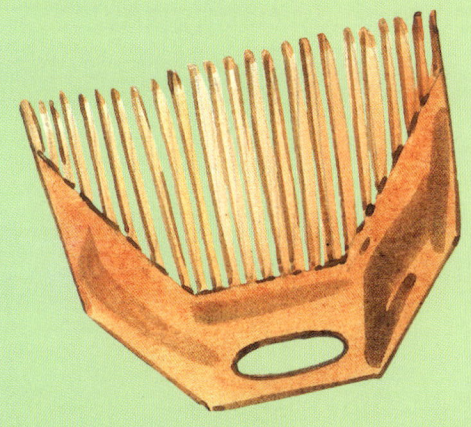

On hearing from Bhai Mardana what Wali Qandhari had told him, Guru Nanak sent him once again to the angry priest, again fetching no fruitful result. The people began to lose hope — Guru Nanak assured them and repeated, "Do not lose heart. God is great and merciful. God can make springs flow from wherever He wishes. Let us all pray to Him." They all prayed and finally Guru Nanak lifted a stone. Lo and behold! A stream of fresh water began to flow from the very spot that Guru Nanak had lifted the stone.

At the same time, Bawa Wali Qandhari's spring dried up. This enraged him further and he pushed a large rock from the top of the hill that came rolling down towards the Guru with lightening speed. The thought that the rock would crush Guru Nanak to instant death made the arrogant priest very happy — but to his utter surprise, Guru Nanak quietly raised his hand and the rock stopped the moment it struck his hand — Guru Nanak's hand (Panja) was imprinted on the rock.

Bawa Wali Qandhari was awe-struck on witnessing the miracle; without wasting any further time, he rushed down the hill and fell at Guru Nanak's feet. Humble as he was, Nanak said, "Rise, my friend. Live as devotees of God should live. Be kind to everyone." Today, the Gurudwara Panja Sahib still stands at that spot, with the huge rock bearing the imprint of Guru Nanak's hand carefully preserved for his followers to see.

Guru Nanak went out on his travels because he had to spread the word of God, as He had told him to do. Just like he did in Mecca and Haridwar, Guru Nanak explained to people about the futility of ritualistic practices that were completely devoid of any spiritual content. He spoke against caste distinctions and idol worship and asked people to place their faith in God alone.

He explained to people about the dangers of egotism, and called upon the people to engage in worship by taking the name of God (Naam Japna). He asked the people to recite and meditate on the name of God (Shabad), believe in the divine order (Hukum), and

also believe in their Guru and his teachings. But Guru Nanak also explained that such worship needed to be selfless (Sewa) and when the people would sing God's name, all their doubts would be discarded and faith would reign supreme.

Guru Nanak continued on his travels for the major portion of his life. He and his followers, including Bhai Mardana, who were being regarded as a separate community by then, greeted each other with the expression "Sat Kartar" (God is True). They lived off the offerings of people, which they also distributed amongst the poor. In the event they had some surplus food and money left with them after feeding the destitute, they would return it to the hosts and ask them to use it to maintain a common kitchen, where people of all races, castes and religions could eat. This practice is continued in Gurudwaras even today, and is known as the Langar.

Through his simple teachings, Guru Nanak asked his disciples to chant the name of God at all times (Naam Japna), earn an honest living without cheating anyone (Kirat Karo) and sharing with others and helping those who were in need of help (Vand Chakko).

Towards the end of his life, Guru Nanak settled down as a peasant farmer at Kartarpur, a small village in Punjab. He would very efficiently divide his day between tending to his farmlands and in offering discourses to all the people who would come to hear him speak.

Guru Nanak was committed to the cause of spreading the message of God and helping people go beyond the age old beliefs that did not help them reach out to God in the first place. And therefore, he named

his successor in Bhai Lehna, who came to be known as Guru Angad, (Angad meaning "a part of you") and was the second Guru of the Sikhs. Guru Nanak died shortly after, in September of 1539 at his home in Kartarpur, at the age of 70.

GURU ANGAD

Born to a prosperous Hindu trader named Bhai Pheru, Bhai Lehna went on to become Guru Angad, the second Sikh Guru. He was born in March, 1504, in the village of Sarae Naga, in the Muktsar district of Punjab. His family moved to Khadur eventually.

Before he became a Sikh, he was an ardent devotee of the Goddess Durga. On one of his visits to the temple of Durga at Jwalamukhi, he came across a Sikh, Bhai Jodha, reciting the Japji, the early morning prayer composed by Guru Nanak.

On hearing about Guru Nanak from Bhai Jodha, Lehna decided to visit the Guru and pay his respects. Upon meeting Guru Nanak at the age of 27, Lehna was convinced that only Guru Nanak could guide him on the path to understanding the ways and methods of God — he became a devout disciple of Guru Nanak and started a new life under the Guru's tutelage. He dedicated himself to the service of Guru Nanak and began to live at Kartarpur. It was time for Guru Nanak to choose his successor. He decided to test his sons and his disciples, before naming his successor.

Though there are many tales and fables as to the kind of tests Guru Nanak tried out on his followers to succeed him, it is believed that once Guru Nanak asked his sons to wash a jug that was covered in mud. Both his sons refused, one saying that he would not get himself dirty trying to clean all that mud on the jug, while the other refused saying that cleaning a dirty jug was below the status of a Guru's son. But Lehna not only cleaned the jug, he also filled it with clean water before presenting it to the Guru.

Another story goes that Guru Nanak was once cutting through a forest with his followers, when suddenly gold and silver coins started pouring around them. All his disciples rushed to grab the coins, but Bhai Lehna and Bhai Buddha remained at the Guru's side. Encouraged by their devotion, Guru Nanak took them to the pyre in the forest and asked them both to eat the corpse lying beneath it. Bhai Buddha could not believe what Guru Nanak had asked them to do and took to his heels, whereas Bhai Lehna immediately went and started removing the wood to carry out his Guru's orders. Beneath the stack of logs, there was no dead body, but a plate full of sweets. Collecting the sweets, he rushed back to Guru Nanak and offered the same to him.

Seeing his loyalty and belief in his Guru's words, Guru Nanak proclaimed Bhai Lehna in his own image, revealed the Japji to him and appointed him as his successor.

Bhai Lehna was renamed Bhai Angad (part of the body) by Guru Nanak in September 1539. After the death of Guru Nanak, Guru Angad became the Second Guru of the Sikhs.

When Guru Nanak left this world, Guru Angad went into meditation for six months — he met no one. Finally, a delegation of Sikhs led by Baba Buddha convinced the Guru that they needed him to show them the way to God.

Guru Angad was a very humble man. He told his disciples that they should strive to remain pure amidst all the impurity in this world. He strictly followed the daily routine followed by Guru Nanak. He earned his own living by twisting coarse grass into strings used for cots. He lived by the code of dignity of menial labour and all the money that he made by making these strings was put into the common fund.

He also popularised the institution of the Langar, a system of community kitchen set up by Guru Nanak where free food was provided to people of all religions and castes. The Guru's own wife too worked in the community kitchen.

Guru Angad was extremely fond of children — he took great interest in their education and around the year, 1541, modified the Punjabi script and introduced the Gurmukhi script. The script became popular among the Sikhs, who till then did not have much knowledge about it. The development of Gurmukhi as a language allowed the Sikhs to have a language of their own and thereby, have their own identity. Moreover, having a separate language of their own, allowed the followers of the Sikh faith to move away from the Sanskrit religious tradition. The modification of the old Punjabi language into Gurmukhi was therefore one of the greatest achievements of Guru Angad's period.

Guru Angad also believed in the fact that along with the development of the mind, physical prowess and strength too needed to be improved amongst the youth — and therefore, he started the Mall Akhara, where young boys would go and play sports and exercise.

In 1544, he wrote a book on Guru Nanak's life and had a number of copies of Guru Nanak's hymns written out in the new Gurmukhi script. Guru Angad increased the number of Sikh religious centers in an attempt to spread Sikhism.

Guru Angad became more and more popular among the people and this led to much jealousy among the Hindu high castes — they were also angry with him because he was preaching a casteless society. They got together to turn the people away from the Guru. So, the year when there was no rain, a Hindu priest told the villagers that despite all their respect and love that they had for Guru Angad, he could not provide rain for their dying crops. He further told them that only when the Guru left the village would there be rainfall. Believing this, the ignorant farmers went to Guru Angad and told him to leave the village as soon as possible. Guru explained to them that nature would not follow such silly superstitions. However, in order to please the villagers he left the village that very instant.

Once away, Guru Angad was refused shelter in neighbouring villages as well, as word spread that he would bring doom to them too. He finally sought shelter in a forest. However, when the rains did not come down in the village as promised, the villagers understood their folly and angry with the evil-minded Hindu priest who had misled them, they punished him by tying him to a plough and dragging him through their fields. The rains finally poured and the farmers begged Guru Angad to return to them. The kind-hearted Guru was very sad on hearing about the punishment meted out to the priest, and told the villagers that they should have been more patient and tolerant toward him and that the wise are always expected to be forgiving and humble in both happiness and sorrow.

Like Guru Nanak, Guru Angad too named his trusted disciple, Sri Amar Das as his successor and the next Sikh Guru. He presented all the holy scripts to Amar Das and also the scripts that he had obtained from Guru Nanak himself. Guru Angad passed away in March 1552, at the age of 47.

GURU AMAR DAS

There lived a very devout Vaishnavite Hindu named Amar Das, who was born in May, 1479. He was the eldest son of Sri Tej Bhan Bhalla, a wealthy farmer and trader in the village of Basarke, near Amritsar in India. As a young man, for over 20 years, he regularly made pilgrimages to the river Ganga for ritual baths. While returning from his twelfth such pilgrimage, he was dumbfounded when a monk he met had asked him a very simple, yet important question — "Who is your Guru?" He could not answer the monk as he did not have an answer. He spent the next few years of his life in looking for his Guru. All his efforts to do so went in vain and Amar Das wandered from place to place without giving up. Then, one day, he heard Bibi Amro, the daughter of Guru Angad, who was recently married to his nephew, singing the holy songs composed by Guru Nanak. Enchanted by the songs to which he listened each day, a curious Amar Das learnt a lot about the mission of Guru Nanak from Bibi Amro, who eventually introduced him to her father, Guru Angad.

Each year, Guru Angad would present a turban as a symbol of honour to his devoted followers. Such was the devotion of Amar Das for his Guru that with the passing of each year he would wear one turban over the other, refusing to discard the previous turbans presented to him by his Guru.

Finding that the humble Amar Das was his most worthy disciple and feeling that it was time for him to name his successor, Guru Angad announced in March 1552 that Amar Das would be his successor. Guru Angad bowed before Guru Amar Das placing five copper coins and a coconut before him just as Guru Nanak had done before declaring him to be the next Guru. Guru Angad then had Baba Buddha put a saffron mark on Guru Amar Das' forehead. Shortly thereafter, Guru Angad left this world on March 29, 1552. Guru Amar Das then became the Third Guru of the Sikhs, at the age of 73.

As the third Guru, Guru Amar Das expanded the institution of free community kitchens called Langar, and made his disciples, whether rich or poor, whether belonging to high caste or low caste, have their meals together, sitting in one place. He thus

    Amar Das soon became a devout disciple of Guru Angad — he served him with great respect, love and passion. One of Guru Angad's wealthy disciples, Gobind, decided to build a new township on the river Beas in honour of Guru Angad. Guru Angad sent Amar Das to supervise the construction of this new township which came to be known as Gowindwal. Once completed, Guru Angad instructed Amar Das to move to Gowindwal with his family, which he did.

    Early each morning, Amar Das would fill a pitcher with the waters of the river Beas and walk with it all the way to Khadur, where Guru Angad lived. Guru Angad used the water for bathing. After serving his Guru the whole day, Amar Das would then return to Gowindwal with the empty pitcher. As a mark of respect to his Guru, while doing so, he never for once turned his back toward Guru Angad. In this way, the most devout disciple of Guru Angad, Amar Das, served his beloved Guru for twelve years at a stretch.

established social equality amongst the people and worked toward strengthening Guru Nanak's principle that believed in all people being the children of God. Anyone who would arrive at a Gurudwara, compulsorily had to sit down at the Langar, before meeting the Guru.

Guru Amar Das also introduced the Anand Karaj marriage ceremony for the Sikhs, replacing the Hindu practice. He tried to free women from the practices of covering their face with a veil and also abolished the practice of sati, which was the system of the Hindu wife setting herself on fire on her husband's funeral pyre. This greatly helped in alleviating the position of women in society.

There are 907 hymns composed by Guru Amar Das that are included in the Guru Granth Sahib. He also created the prayer ritual called Anand Sahib, which is one of the Five Banis recited daily, even today.

Guru Amar Das passed away in September 1574, after naming Bhai Jetha, his younger son-in-law, as his successor. After his death Bhai Jetha came to be known as Guru Ram Das and was the Fourth Guru of the Sikhs.

GURU RAM DAS

Ram Das was born in Lahore, on September 24, 1534, to very honest and pious parents. As a child he was fondly called Jetha, being the first-born of his parents. As a kid he was very rarely seen crying and almost always went about with a smile on his face.

The village Basarke, which was the native place of the third Guru, Guru Amar Das, was also the village from where Jetha's mother came. When Jetha was seven years old, his father died. His maternal then took him to Basarke. There, he grew up to be a handsome young man. One day, Guru Amar Das happened to see him and was so impressed with Jetha's sense of devotion and polite manners that he instantly decided to get his second daughter, Bibi Bhani, married to him.

Bibi Bhani served Jetha not merely as her dear husband, but also as a revered saint. With the passage of time, Ram Das moved with his family to Gowindwal, where Bibi Bhani's father, Guru Amar Das lived.

Soon after, a small group of Hindus approached Emperor Akbar in Lahore and complained to him that Guru Amar Das was condemning Hindu practices and preaching against casteism and idol worship. Hearing the complaint, the Emperor called for Guru Amar Das and sought an explanation. Due to failing health and old age, Guru Amar Das excused himself and instead sent Bhai Ram Das to address the allegations made against him in court. Guru Amar Das ensured him that Guru Nanak was always with him and would help him if the need arose.

Bhai Ram Das appeared at the Mughal court and answered all the charges leveled against his Guru in the complaint to the complete satisfaction of the Emperor. Greatly pleased with the skill and confidence with which he cleared all the charges, the Emperor dismissed the complaint outright and requested Bhai Jetha to convey his deep respects to the Guru — such was the calm and composed nature of Ram Das!

Bhai Jetha was an image of love, devotion, service and resignation. He looked upon Guru Amar Das not merely as his father-in-law, but more as his respected Guru. He surrendered himself to him. He, along with his wife, Bibi Bhani, used to draw water, bathe him, cook, serve him meals from the kitchen and then wash the dishes. The more he served his Guru, the more Bhai Jetha's love for him and for all mankind increased. Gradually, he became more and more saintly and shone with divine light.

Later on, when the construction of the baoli or 'well' at Gowindwal was undertaken, Ram Das worked very hard and even went to the extent of carrying baskets of earth on his head. This annoyed his relatives no end, who thought that he was engaging himself in menial work way below the level of the Guru's son-in-law — yet, Bhai Jetha was determined to serve his Guru and mankind.

The final and supreme test of Jetha's spirit of service and sacrifice came when Guru Amar Das wanted to select his successor. The Guru asked both his sons-in-law, Rama and Jetha, to erect two platforms beside the baoli. He promised to honour the one who would do better work according to him, without leaking out the secret that he was in fact, looking for the next Sikh Guru. When they completed their platforms, on inspection, Guru Amar Das

declared both the platforms to be defective. He ordered them to be broken and rebuilt.

However, the new ones were also disapproved by the Guru and he ordered that they be dismantled again and redone. Hearing this, the elder son-in-law, Rama, was disgusted and refused to build it a third time, saying that Guru Amar Das had become old and senile. But, the obedient Bhai Jetha continued to build platforms, one after another without questioning his Guru's judgment even for once. Ultimately, when he still could not satisfy his Guru, with folded hands he bowed before him and told him that he was but a fool who did not possess the knowledge and wisdom of his Guru and begged him to show him the way.

On hearing this, Guru Amar Das smiled and hugged him affectionately announcing that Jetha was the perfect being, the only one who would lead the Sikhs after him. Thus, in 1574, Bhai Jetha succeeded Guru Amar Das as the Fourth Sikh Guru, and was rechristened Ram Das, by Guru Amar Das.

Guru Ram Das founded the city of Ramdaspur, which later came to be known as Amritsar, where he started the construction of the famous Golden Temple, thus making Amritsar the most holy city of the Sikhs. He requested the Muslim Sufi, Mian Mir to lay the cornerstone of the Harmandir Sahib or the Golden Temple that goes to show he had respect for all religions. The temple was made to remain open on all sides and at all times to everyone, thereby signifying that the Sikhs believe only in One God, who is not partial to any particular place, direction or time.

Lawan, the four stanza hymn recited at the Sikh marriage ceremony, Anand Karaj, was also composed by Guru Ram Das.

Guru Ram Das did a lot to uphold the teachings of the Gurus before him and solidified the presence of the Sikh faith in society. He passed away in September 1581 in Amritsar, after naming his eldest son Arjan Dev his successor.

GURU ARJAN DEV

Born in 1563, Arjan Dev was the youngest son of the Fourth Sikh Guru, Guru Ram Das and went on to succeed his father as the Fifth Sikh Guru.

Guru Arjan Dev was appointed as the fifth Sikh Guru in September 1581. As a child, Arjan Dev exhibited good behaviour and wisdom. He spent the first eleven years of his life at Goindwaland then left for Amritsar. The period of Sikhism under the leadership of Guru Arjan Dev is considered to be one of the strongest periods ever, as Sikhism became established as a proper religion, with growing number of people becoming followers of the faith.

Guru Arjan Dev completed the development of Amritsar and it was during his time that the Golden Temple was constructed as well. Bhai Buddha was appointed as the chief priest of the Golden Temple, and Amritsar became the holy land of the believers of the Sikh faith.

Another very important contribution of Guru Arjan Dev was the composition of the Adi Granth, one of the holy books of the Sikhs. The Adi Granth is a collection of the works of the first four Gurus of Sikhism, which Guru Arjan Dev wrote in verse form in 1604. The Adi Granth is one of the very few religious texts that have still survived over time in their original handwritten form. Guru Arjan Dev placed the Adi Granth on what was his seat at the Golden Temple and himself sat on the floor with all the other common people who came to seek blessings at the holy temple.

Guru Arjan Dev was also credited with having founded the cities of Taran Taran and Kartarpur. To ease the sufferings of the people, Guru Arjan Dev even helped in the construction of a baoli, or well, in Lahore. To irrigate fields, Guru Arjan Dev also helped farmers build six-wheel Persian wells.

Guru Arjan Dev also started another very important practice when he organised the Masand system, wherein a group of representatives went around cities, towns and villages, spreading the words and teachings of the Sikh Gurus. They also collected Dasvand — one tenth of the earnings of every Sikh, which went to maintain the Langar at the Golden Temple.

The land of Amritsar was given to the Sikhs as a jagir, which was the Mughal system of gifting land to individuals for some good deeds done by them. Emperor Akbar offered this land to the Sikhs since he was extremely impressed by the practice of the Langar. He himself ate once at the Langar, seated with the common folk on the floor.

Guru Arjan Dev dealt in horses to earn his own personal living, and thereby he set an example to people to be as zealous in trade as they were in religion. Things like these helped the teachings of Guru Nanak take a firm hold on the followers of Sikhism. He asked his followers to preserve their faith on the teachings of the Sikh Gurus before him and therefore, believe in the equality of man, in the equality between man and woman, in the equality of work and the need to work and to respect all religions. After all, the foundation stone for the Golden Temple was laid by a Muslim fakir!

However, the Mughal Emperor Jahangir, Akbar's son, was upset with the fact that more and more Muslims were converting to Sikhism after hearing the words and teachings of Guru Nanak and the other Sikh Gurus. Emperor Jahangir was not as tolerant of other religions as his father, Emperor Akbar. He did not approve of mass conversions of followers of Islam to Sikhism. It is believed that he ordered for the arrest and consequent execution of Guru Arjan Dev.

Due to the unjust reasons of his death, some sources suggest that Guru Arjan Singh passed himself on to his son, Hargobind, who was then anointed as his successor and the Sixth Guru of the Sikhs.

GURU HARGOBIND

Born in 1595, Hargobind was the son of the Fifth Sikh Guru, Guru Arjan Dev. He was named as the successor by his father, Guru Arjan Dev, and with the death of his father he became the Sixth Guru of the Sikhs in May 1606.

Guru Hargobind was only eleven at the time of his father's death, who had been imprisoned and executed by the Mughal Emperor Jahangir, owing to religious intolerance. Guru Hargobind was naturally on a war-path against the Mughals from the time he was annointed the Sixth Sikh Guru.

After the injustice that was meted out to his father, Guru Hargobind knew very clearly that he would have to defend the Sikhs against the Mughals and other such forces who wished harm for the followers of the Sikh faith. Therefore, with his becoming the Sixth Guru of the Sikhs, the entire Sikh community was converted into a warrior race. Guru Hargobind himself carried two swords

at all times — one of them was named Miri, which represented the Guru's political command over his people as their leader, and the other one was called Piri, which signified his spiritual power over his people as their religious Guru.

Guru Hargobind knew that his people too would have to learn how to defend themselves, and he encouraged them to maintain their physical fitness. Guru Hargobind himself was brilliant in Shastravidya (Martial Arts) and set a fine example for his people to follow.

The Guru also built a Risaldari, or an army, with seven hundred horses, three hundred horsemen and sixty gunners with time. The need for armed counter-measures for attacks against Sikhs was foreseen by Guru Arjan Dev and understood by Guru Hargobind. The number of infantry kept rising over the years. Guru Hargobind also built a fortress called Lohgarh, which meant 'A Fortress of Steel'.

Moreover, the Guru also had a retinue of sixty matchlock men acting as bodyguards which formed the nucleus of his future army.

The Mughal Emperor Jahangir was not very pleased with Guru Hargobind for arming the Sikh people as a whole, as that was a direct challenge to his political rule. He therefore, had Guru Hargobind arrested and imprisoned at the Gwalior Fort. He was released soon after, but Guru Hargobind demanded that his fellow Sikhs, who had been imprisoned along with him, be released too. This incident however, went on to strain relations between the Mughals and the Sikhs even further.

Along with Guru Arjan Dev's fiscal policies and Guru Hargobind's martial policy, this period saw, instead, the rise of the Sikhs into a separate and identifiable community. The number of Sikhs also increased manifold during this time.

Guru Hargobind was also responsible for the creation of the Akal Takht, which in the English language meant "Throne of the Almighty". The Akal Takht was one of the seats of religious and political authority of the Sikhs and is located at the Harmandir Sahib Complex in Amritsar. Akal in Gurumukhi refers to the "timeless one", or "God", and Takht meant "seat".

Physical feats were performed in the courtyard before the Akal Takht. Visitors were received and complaints were heard and redressed. Under Guru Hargobind was also established the custom of choirs moving at night around the Golden Temple. This coustom is followed till today.

After ushering in one of the most glorious periods of Sikhism, Guru Hargobind breathed his last at Kiratpur in March 1644.

GURU HAR RAI

Before his death, Guru Hargobind had nominated his grandson, Har Rai, as his successor. Therefore, with the death of Guru Hargobind in 1644, Guru Har Rai was anointed the Seventh Guru of the Sikhs.

Guru Har Rai was a very peace-loving man. It is believed that whenever his robe would flow over some plants and trample them, he would get very upset and it would take him a long time to get back his peace of mind.

But, even though he was gentle, he was a very able fighter and could defend the Sikhs in the face of any emergency. Undoubtedly a peace-loving man, Guru Har Rai also knew the importance of wars and thus, he did not disband the mammoth army that his grandfather, Guru Hargobind, had left behind. Instead he made it grow stronger and larger. During his time, 2200 mounted soldiers were kept in battle-ready state at all times.

An incident states that once when Guru Har Rai was coming back from the Malwa and Doaba regions, where he had carried out some extensive work setting up Sikh missionaries, he was attacked by Mohammad Yarbeg Khan. Yarbeg's father Mukhlis Khan had been killed by Guru Hargobind Singh in a battle earlier. Seeking revenge for his father's death, Mohammad Yarbeg Khan attacked the small two hundred strong Sikh contingent with almost thousand soldiers. But Guru Har Rai and his men turned the enemy inside out and were victorious in the battle.

When Dara Sikoh, the eldest son of the Mughal Emperor Shah Jahan, had been imprisoned by his younger brother Aurangzeb, so that the latter could succeed his father to the Mughal throne, it was Guru Har Rai who helped rescue Dara Sikoh from prison. Much later, when Dara Sikoh had fallen very ill, and physicians from even

abroad could not help him in any way, Shah Jahan approached Guru Har Rai for help. Guru Har Rai, who was very well versant with homeopathic medicines, offered Dara Sikoh some herbs and within the next few days, he completely cured of his illness.

However, when his followers asked the Guru as to why he had helped the enemy who was responsible for the death of Guru Arjan Dev and who had fought numerous battles against his grandfather, Guru Hargobind, Guru Har Rai merely replied, "When the axe cuts through the sandal tree, the perfume of the sandal tree remains on the axe. So should a Guru always return good for evil."

Guru Har Rai did a lot to reform the Masand system, which had been started by Guru Arjan Dev to spread the teachings of the Sikh Gurus and had been corrupted by power hungry Sikhs over time. During his time, he established around 350 Sikh Missionaries, which were known as Manji.

When his eldest son, Ram Rai, distorted the Sikh prayer, Bani, before the Mughal Emperor Aurangzeb, Guru Har Rai was saddened at his son's lack of courage and disowned him. Before passing away in 1661, Guru Har Rai nominated his youngest son, Har Krishan to be the next Guru after him, when he was just five years old.

GURU HAR KRISHAN

Born in July 1656 at Kiratpur, Guru Har Krishan was the youngest son of the Seventh Sikh Guru, Guru Har Rai and was also the youngest Guru of the Sikhs ever, when he became the Eighth Guru of the Sikhs at the age of five.

Since his elder brother, Ram Rai, had distorted the Sikh prayer, Bani, before the Mughal Emperor Aurangzeb, Guru Har Rai had ex-communicated him and had named Guru Har Krishan as his successor.

Guru Har Krishan was only five years old when he was anointed as the Eighth Sikh Guru. His initial challenge, even at that young age, came from his own elder brother, Ram Rai, who had moved to the Mughal court of Aurangzeb to help him become the next Guru by overthrowing his own younger brother.

Aurangzeb naturally wanted Ram Rai as the Guru of the Sikhs and therefore sent an emissary to Raja Jai Singh, a strong Sikh

and a devotee of the Guru. When Guru Har Krishan arrived at the Mughal Emperor's court in Delhi, Aurangzeb offered him two plates — one full of ornaments and toys, and the other held a holy man's cloak and bowl. Aurangzeb was humbled when Guru Har Krishan accepted the second plate instead of the first.

When he was in Delhi, Guru Har Krishan was staying at Raja Jai Singh's palace, at a place called Bangla Sahib. It was during his stay in Delhi, even as people came from all over the country to pay their respects to the Guru, there was an outbreak of small pox and cholera. There were thousands dying because of the epidemic.

Guru Har Krishan immediately started helping the people who were suffering from small pox. The lake at Bangla Sahib, behind Raja Jai Singh's palace was purified by Guru Har Krishan and as people drank that water and washed themselves with it, they were miraculously cured. Without making any distinction of race, caste and religion, Guru Har Krishan continuously served the people and helped them cure themselves.

But it was during his efforts to help the people against cholera and small pox, the young Guru contracted the disease himself. But in spite of his ill health, the Guru did not deter in serving the people. His own health kept failing with every passing day.

Seeing the poor state that he was in, his mother asked him how he, the individual who sat on the throne of Guru Nanak and dispelled the diseases of people, could be so near to his own death. The young Guru replied that while the throne of Guru Nanak was immortal, the mortal body who sat on it would have to suffer sickness and disease, as it was a part of life.

Even though Guru Har Krishan did not lead a long life, he lived a wise and fruitful life, carrying out Guru Nanak's teachings in practice. When he was very close to his death, Guru Har Krishan mumbled, "Bakala". This was interpreted as the Guru nominating an individual from the town of Bakala as his successor. It was understood that Guru Har Krishan had named Teg Bahadur, his grand uncle as his successor.

Finally, in April 1664, Guru Har Krishan passed away, being the youngest Guru to have ever vacated the throne of the Gurus.

GURU TEG BAHADUR

The Eighth Sikh Guru, Guru Har Krishan was very young when he passed away in April 1664. However, before he breathed his last, he did indicate that his successor would be someone from the town of Bakala. It was then that the granduncle of the deceased Sikh Guru, Teg Bahadur became the new and the Ninth Guru of the Sikhs.

Guru Teg Bahadur was born with the name Tyag Mal, and was the son of the Sixth Sikh Guru, Guru Hargobind. It was from his father that he had mastered the art of sword fighting, and when he was only thirteen years old, he had accompanied his father, Guru Hargobind in battle. Not only had the Sikhs won the war with the Mughals, Tyag Mal had displayed great prowess with the sword, and even at that early age, he had slain many soldiers of the invading army. It was because of his feat during the battle that he was given the name Teg Bahadur, which roughly translated means 'The Brave Sword Wielder'.

Even from that young age, Guru Teg Bahadur had displayed all the signs of being the next Guru after his father. He would meditate for long hours and concentrated on his studies. By 1632, he was married to Mata Gujri at Kartarpur.

However, with the passing of his son, Bhai Gurditta, Guru Hargobind started grooming his grandson, Guru Har Rai to be the next Guru of the Sikhs after him. When his wife had asked whether her own son, Guru Teg Bahadur would be the next Guru or not, Guru Hargobind had replied that Guru Teg Bahadur would one day surely become the Guru of the Sikhs. He even prophesied that, Guru Teg Bahadur and his son would be the greatest Gurus in their fight for justice in the country.

Guru Hargobind then asked Guru Teg Bahadur to move to Bakala with his family and reside there. In Bakala, Guru Teg Bahadur spent almost the next twenty years in an underground room, lost in meditation.

During the last days of Guru Har Krishan, a merchant ship was passing through a storm. The captain of the vessel, a devout Sikh merchant, prayed that if he were to reach land safe and sound, he would make an offering of 500 gold coins to the Sikh Guru.

Therefore, when he landed on the shore, he at once started moving towards Delhi to keep his vow. But while still on the way to Delhi, he heard the news that Guru Har Krishan had passed away and had said that his successor would be found in the town of Bakala. Without wasting any more time, the merchant started travelling to Bakala, to find the next Guru and give him the 500 gold coins.

But on reaching Bakala, the merchant was shocked to see that 22 members of the Sodhi dynasty that lived there were all claiming to be the next Sikh Guru. Since Guru Har Krishan had not named any particular individual, but had just indicated that his successor would be found in Bakala, the members of the Sodhi dynasty, one of the most influential families in Bakala, were all propping themselves up as the next Guru.

Not knowing how to keep to his pledge, now that there were 22 Sikh Gurus, the merchant decided to give each of the self-proclaimed Gurus two gold coins. But just as he was about to leave after completing his deed, he learnt that there was one more saint, who had been meditating for nearly twenty years. The merchant went to him as well and left his two gold coins at the feet of this sage. The sage only replied, "Why are you going back on your word now? You said you would give 500 gold coins to the Guru!"

The man came running back to the streets yelling that he had found the Ninth Sikh Guru.

Guru Teg Bahadur maintained the splendour of the Guru's court that had been in practice since the time of Guru Hargobind, and even maintained a private army like before. However, he did not

engage in war with any sect or political power during his time as the Guru. He merely met all his disciples and followers and gave them his blessings and explained the ways and teachings of the Sikh Gurus. And though he maintained the pomp and splendour of a Guru's court, he lived his private life very austerely.

He started the construction of a city in Himachal Pradesh, after being gifted the land by Rani Champa of Bilaspur. While he had named the city Chakk Nanaki, this city later came to be called Anandpur, meaning 'The City of Bliss' and was the site were the Sikh religion later went through one of its greatest transformations.

Soon after, he set off for all the holy places that had earlier been visited by Guru Nanak. He travelled through Uttar Pradesh, Bihar, Bengal and through what is now known as Bangladesh. It was when he was moving through Patna that his son, Gobind Rai was born. He would later go on to be one of the most influential Sikh Gurus, Guru Gobind Singh.

Guru Teg Bahadur was received warmly at all the places he visited, where he gave discourses and encouraged the Sikh faith in people. He kept the teachings of Guru Nanak alive through letter and spirit during his travels. For instance, when he reached Kurukshetra, there was an eclipse that day and the brahmins present there, told him to take a bath in the sacred tank to cleanse himself. Guru Teg Bahadur replied that taking a bath in a sacred tank cannot wash away sins, because the mind cannot be touched by water. Only with absolute belief in the Almighty can someone become pure.

Meanwhile, the Mughal Emperor Aurangzeb had started a religious feud and was converting Hindus to Islam. He ransacked temples, destroyed them and forced the people to accept Islam as their new faith. Soon, his evil intentions reached Kashmir, where Aurangzeb decided to convert the revered Brahmin Pundits of Kashmir. Not knowing what to do, the Kashmiri Pundits turned to Guru Teg Bahadur for help.

Guru Teg Bahadur knew that the only way in which this religious massacre could end was if a holy man would lay down his life to stop the atrocities. He therefore anointed his son, Gobind Singh as the next Guru after him and as the Tenth Guru of the Sikhs, and went to Delhi to appeal to Aurangzeb.

Aurangzeb too had understood that Guru Teg Bahadur alone could cause him some problems and therefore had the Guru arrested. After brutal torturing, Guru Teg Bahadur was executed by beheading by the Mughals. His disciples managed to escape with the Guru's lifeless body and had him cremated, lest the Mughals get hold of the Guru's body. One of his disciples, Bhai Lakhi Shah, carried the Guru's body to his own house and set the whole house on fire to protect the Guru. At the site of this house now stands Gurudwara Rakab Ganj Sahib, 'rakab' meaning 'ashes'. The place where he was executed is now Gurudwara Sis Ganj. Both the Gurudwaras are in Delhi.

Guru Teg Bahadur's noble sacrifice was in the true nature of Sikh values. With his death, his son, Guru Gobind Singh, became the Tenth Guru of the Sikhs.

GURU GOBIND SINGH

Born Gobind Rai Sodhi in December 1666, in Patna, Bihar. Guru Gobind Singh went on to become the Tenth Sikh Guru and one of the most influential Gurus of the Sikhs. On the site of his house at Patna, where he was born and where he spent his early childhood, now stands a sacred shrine, Takht Sri Patna Sahib, one of the five most honoured religious seats for the Sikhs.

When Gobind Rai was around six years old, his family shifted to Anandpur, in Punjab, where his early education included reading and writing of Punjabi, Braj, Sanskrit and Persian. He was barely nine years of age when his father met a tragic end at the hands of the Mughal Emperor, Aurangzeb. Gobind Singh was then formally installed as Guru in March 1676.

Besides dedicating his life to the concerns of his community and followers, Guru Gobind Singh gave much attention to sports, physical exercise and education. With a natural talent for writing

poetry, the young Guru spent much of his time composing poems, songs and verses that mainly depicted battle or war themes in order to instill the fighting spirit amongst his followers so as to enable them to stand up against injustice and tyranny.

Guru Gobind Singh had shifted to Paonta, on the banks of the river Yamuna, in the year 1685. He wrote and composed most of his works there, through which he preached love and equality and how to lead a life full of discipline, honesty and morality. He taught the worship of the One Supreme Being, discouraging praying before idols and the following of superstitious beliefs.

While preaching glorification of the sword, he stressed that the sword was never meant to be a symbol of aggression, and it was never to be used for selfish reasons — rather, it was the emblem of courage and self-respect and was to be used only in self-defence, when all other means of protecting oneself had failed.

During his stay at Paonta, Guru Gobind Singh used his spare time to practice different forms of exercises, such as riding, swimming and archery. His people followed him and soon, the Guru and his people became a martially strong force to reckon with — on several occasions they defeated the invading Rajputs and Mughals.

Guru Gobind Singh was receiving complaints about the dishonest practices of the Masands or the local ministers of the religious centres. He issued directions to the Sikh communities in different places to ignore the corrupt Masands and instead come in person, directly to Anandpur with their offerings. The Guru thus established a direct relationship with his Sikh followers and addressed them as his Khalsa.

The institution of the Khalsa was officially recognised in March 1699, when Sikhs had gathered at Anandpur in large numbers for the annual festival of Baisakhi. On this day, Guru Gobind Singh appeared before the crowd and with a bare sword in hand, dramatically asked whether there was a true Sikh amidst the assembly who was willing to offer his head to the Guru as a sacrifice! The people present were stunned and there was pin-drop silence for the next few minutes.

The Guru repeated the question, and only after he made the third call did Daya Ram, a Sobti Khatri of Lahore, come forward. He humbly walked behind the Guru to a tent nearby and after some time the Guru returned with his sword dripping blood, when he asked for another head. At this, Dharam Das, a Jat from Hastinapur, came forward and was once again taken inside the same tent. In this way Guru Gobind Singh made three more calls, each time returning from the enclosure with his blood-stained sword.

Muhkam Chand, a washerman from Dwarka, Himmat, a water-carrier from Jagannath Puri, and Sahib Chand, a barber from Bidar responded one after another and advanced to offer their heads. All the five were later led back from the tent, alive, all dressed in saffron-coloured clothes, and with neatly tied turbans of similar hue on their heads. They had swords dangling by their sides.

Then, Guru Gobind Singh blessed the five chosen Sikhs and introduced them to the crowd present there, as Panj Piare, the five devoted spirits who were the beloved of the Guru — these five were the first to be baptised to the order of the Khalsa. All of them, bearing the surname Singh, meaning lion, were required to wear in future the five symbols of the Khalsa, all beginning with the letter 'K' — namely, Kesh or long hair and beard, Kangha or comb in the kesh to keep it tidy, Kara or steel bracelet on the wrist, Kachchha or short breeches and Kirpan or sword. It was also decided that the women would henceforth bear the surname Kaur, meaning 'princess'.

The Khalsa was thus set up by the Guru, in whom he invested the final authority to protect the helpless and fight the oppressor and to

preach the principles of Sikhism. On the Guru's insistence, the Khalsa baptised him into the order and at the same time, changed his name from Guru Gobind Rai to Guru Gobind Singh. Further instructions were laid down for the Sikhs — they could never cut or trim their hair and beard, nor smoke tobacco. A Sikh must be faithful to his wife and family and refrain from eating the flesh of an animal killed slowly in the Muslim way or in any sacrificial ceremony.

These developments annoyed the caste-ridden Rajput chiefs of the Sivalik hills. They got together and convinced Emperor Aurangzeb to rise against the Guru and his followers. The Sikhs put up a valiant fight against them. After a point of time, the Mughals, swearing by the Quran, promised the Guru and his men a safe passage while leaving Anandpur. However, the Sikhs were betrayed by the Mughals later, who attacked them and overpowered them with only the Guru, his two sons and five Sikhs being in a position to flee Anandpur. All the others fell to their deaths.

Guru Gobind Singh's two younger sons, Zorawar Singh and Fateh Singh, along with his mother, Mata Gujri, were, after the evacuation of Anandpur, betrayed by their old servant and escort, Gangu, who deceitfully took them to the enemy and had the young children executed on December 13, 1705, along with their grandmother.

Tired and saddened by the death of his followers and his family, Guru Gobind Singh continued to wander fearlessly from place to place, until he again came face to face with his enemies who had been chasing him all this while — a great fight followed, and despite the

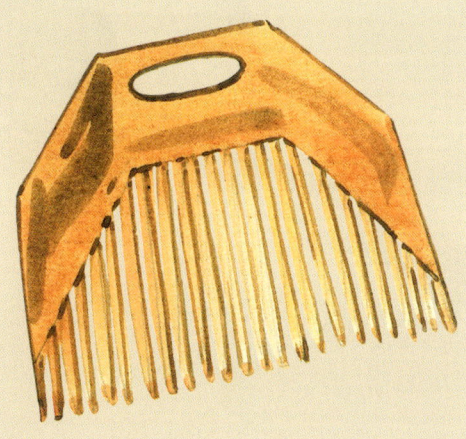

overwhelming number of the Mughal troops, they failed to capture the Guru and had to retire in defeat.

After spending some time in forests, Guru Gobind Singh finally arrived at Talwandi Sabo, now called Damdama Sahib, in January 1706. During his stay there of over nine months, a number of Sikhs rejoined him. It was here that he revised the Sikh scripture, the Guru Granth Sahib, with the help of the celebrated scholar, Bhai Mani Singh.

After Emperor Aurangzeb's death, Guru Gobind Singh sided with the Emperor's eldest son, Bahadur Shah and helped him fight his younger brother from claiming the throne. After Bahadur Shah became Emperor, his respect and love for the Guru grew more and more and this angered Nawab Wazir Khan of Sirhind, who became jealous of the Emperor's growing friendship with Guru Gobind Singh.

Burning with envy, the Nawab entrusted two of his faithful men with murdering the Guru. These two Pathans followed the Guru secretly and arrested him one day at Nanded, where one of them stabbed the Guru right below the heart. Before he could receive

another blow, Guru Gobind Singh struck the Pathan down with his sword, while his fleeing companion was killed by the other Sikhs who had rushed to the spot on hearing the noise.

As the bad news reached Bahadur Shah's camp, the Emperor immediately arranged to send expert British surgeons to attend on the Guru. The wound was stitched and appeared to have healed quickly, but as the Guru one day applied strength to pull a stiff bow, it broke out again and the wound began to bleed profusely. This weakened the Guru very much and the saint-soldier breathed his last in October 1708.

Before the end came, Guru Gobind Singh had asked for the sacred Sri Guru Granth Sahib to be brought before him. His obedient disciple, Daya Singh, brought forth the sacred book. The Guru placed before it a coin and a coconut and bowed his head before it, in the same way a successor was anointed. He then said to the Sikhs present that as per his orders, they should treat the Guru Granth Sahib as their next Guru after he had left this world.

Guru Gobind Singh thus passed on the succession, with due ceremony, to the Holy Book, the Guru Granth Sahib, ending the line of individual Gurus. He told his followers that the spirit of the Guru would henceforth be in the Granth and the Khalsa. "Where the Granth is with any five Sikhs representing the Khalsa, there will the Guru be," he said.

After the demise of Guru Gobind Singh, the Guru Granth Sahib became for all time to come, the Guru for the Sikhs, for the words of the Holy Book were, indeed, the words of the Divine that were revealed to the people by the Gurus.

TITLES IN THIS SERIES

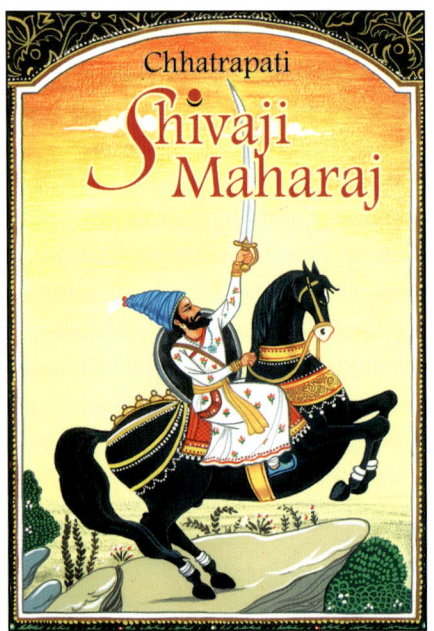

ISBN: 978-93-81607-22-0

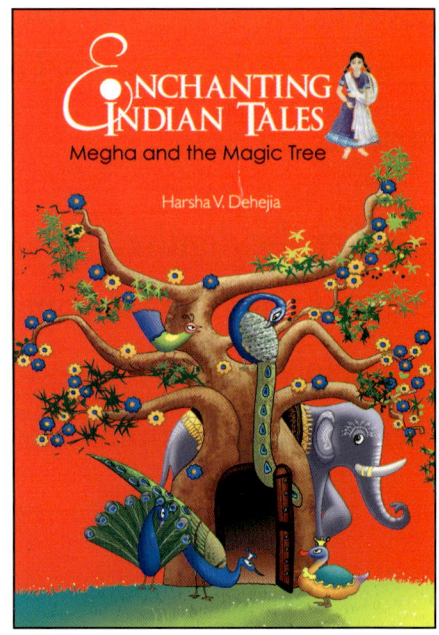

ISBN: 978-93-81607-34-3

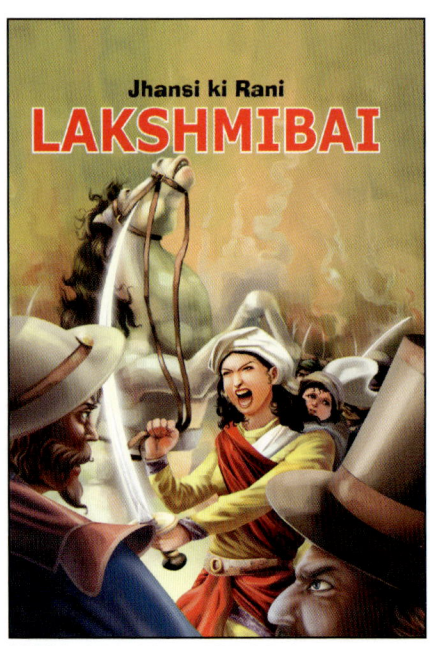

ISBN: 978-93-81607-35-0

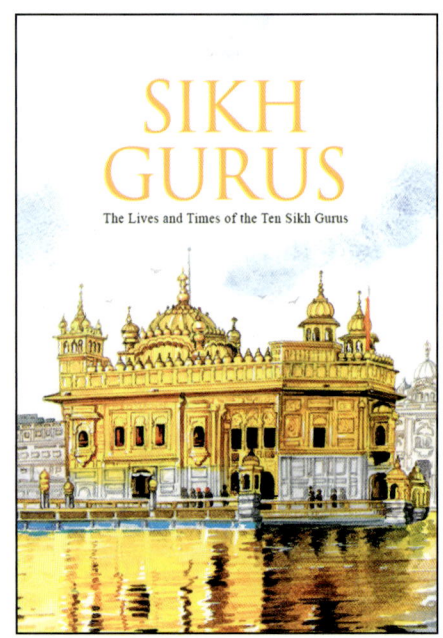

ISBN: 978-93-81607-43-5